The Four Horsemen Prese

ANTHOCON

The Anthology

Conference 2015

June 5 - 7
Portsmouth, New Hampshire

A Celebration of Speculative Fiction, Art, and
the Convergence of Both

Readings

Panels

Workshops

Art Show

AnthoJam

Sponsors

The Four Horsemen would not be able to pull this off without support from our sponsors. We offer them our sincere gratitude.

Sam Adams

Twisted Tea

Prelude Restaurant 7 Ayers Village, Methuen MA

Larry Comics 65 Lakeview, Lowell MA

Rena Mason

Andrew Wolter

Contents

Horsemen's Legion Members for 2015

Michael Bailey
Erich Bruning (2013)
Edward Brzychcy
Dianna Catt
Alice Day
Thom Erb (2012, 2013)
Michelle Erb (2012, 2013)
Dan Foley (2013)
Marianne Halbert (2013)
Bracken MacLeod (2013)
Chris Marrs
Rena Mason
John M. McIlveen
Bob Meracle
Michelle Mixell
G. Elmer Munson
Errick Nunnally
David Price
Kristi Peterson Schoonover
Rob Smales
Mike J. Smith (2013)
Tony Tremblay (2012, 2013)
Sherri White
Andrew Wolter

WELCOME

Welcome to the fourth Anthology Conference in beautiful and historical Portsmouth, NH. The Four Horsemen are pleased and honored that you could join us for what has proven to be a lively and close-knit celebration of the creative arts. This will be the first year of the new Spring dates for the conference, and it is our hope that you will be able to enjoy the sites that Seacoast, New Hampshire has to offer during this time of year.

Those of you who have attended AnthoCon before will note a slight difference in our scheduling. This will be the first year in which most events do not run concurrently. This year we are placing as much emphasis on author readings as we are on panels and workshops. This translates into more readings and a slight (reduction) in other programs. We felt that you should not have to choose between a readings and a panel. Conversely, we did not want authors and panelists to have to compete for your time. We hope that the new scheduling format will maximize the attendance at all conference functions, as well as maximize your enjoyment of the event.

We'd like to thank a number of people for making this event the success we know it will be. Our Minions (volunteers) have worked hard to prepare for the event, and will no doubt be scurrying around the con floor to insure that it runs smoothly — Candace Yost, Michelle Erb, Kira Trudell, and Kevin Lucia. Thanks to Susan Scofield, our artist guest of honor, for tirelessly coordinating the juried art exhibit. Thanks to our panelists, moderators, and workshop members for sharing their knowledge and experience. A huge thanks to our special guests, and thanks to you for supporting another AnthoCon.

Here's hoping you find fun and friendship at our "little" event.

— The Four Horsemen: Mark, jOhnny, Tim, and…

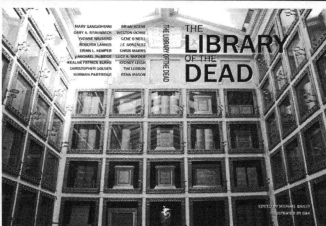

2015 AnthoCon Schedule

Friday:

Dealer load in 6:00 PM
Registration opens at 2:00

7:00 - 11:00 Table 21 Lounge Mixer (Cash bar)

NEW: 7:15 - 8:00 Mixer Roundtable — Pseudonyms - The Life of Two Authors with Andrew Wolter
NEW: 8:00 - 8:45 Mixer Roundtable — Writing Media Tie-ins with Christopher Golden & James A. Moore
NEW: 9:30 - 10:30 Late Night Book Release — THROUGH A MIRROR, DARKLY, Kevin Lucia.

Mixer Roundtables are lively informal discussions held within the Table 21 Lounge & Restaurant over drinks and good company. They are first-come/first served with limited seating.

NEW: 8:00 -12:00 — Call of Cthulhu RPG with DB Poirier (limit 8 people and must sign up in advance at the registration desk).

Saturday:

8:00 - 9:00 Early Bird Panel: Going it Alone — Independent/Self/Hybrid Publishing Strategies

9:00 – 10:00   Readings: Anthology, Year Three: Distant Dying Ember (Michelle Mixelle, Rob Smales, Andrew Wolter etc.)

10:00 - 11:00: Con welcome and Special Guest Panel: State of the Union for Speculative Fiction and Art

11:00 -12:00 Readings: James Moore, Holly Newstein, Stacey Longo, Anthony Tremblay

12:00 – 1:30 Break/Lunch/Shopping

1:30 – 2:30 Readings: Christopher Golden, Bracken Mcleod, Doung Jai Piscitelli, April Hawks

2:30 - 3:30 Group Signings/Book Releases (special releases and readings by Thom Erb and Andrew Wolter)

3:30 – 4:30 Readings: Kristi Petersen Schoonover, Larissa Glasser, Jacob Haddon, Monica O'Rourke

4:30 - 5:30 Panel: Anthologies: editing/constructing/themes

5:30 - 6:30 Readings/Releases: AT THE LAZY K, Gene O'Neill/Written Backwards Anthologies release: THE LIBRARY OF THE DEAD/QUALIA NOUS/CHIRAL MAD with Tom Monteleone, Christopher Golden, et. al

6:30 - 7:00 Tom Monteleone Reading

7:00 - ? AnthoJam/Dinner: Remember that the Saturday night event requires a deluxe ticket, weekend pass, or Horsemen's Legion pass.

Sunday:

Dealer Floor Open 10:00 - 3:30

9:30 - 10:00 Pre-workshop Reading: Gene O'Neill

10:00 - 11:00 Workshop: Gene O'Neill, Autobiography in Fiction

11:00 – 12:00 Readings: NEHW anthology

12:00 – 1:00 Break/Lunch/Shopping

1:00 – 1:30 Readings: Firbolg Publishing

1:30 – 2:30 Readings: Great Old Ones Publishing - From The Corner of Your Eye

2:30 - 3:30 Panel: Business savvy: understanding contracts/preventing exploitation

3:30 Dealer floor closes / Con closing ceremony in Dealer Room

SAMUEL ADAMS®

Workshops and Panels

Mixer Roundtables (Friday Night)

Mixer Roundtables are lively informal discussions held within the Table 21 Lounge & Restaurant over drinks and good company. They are first-come/first served with limited seating. *All Mixer Roundtables require a weekend or day pass to attend.*

Mixer Roundtable — Pseudonyms - The Life of Two Authors with Andrew Wolter

A discussion with Andrew Wolter, AKA "Tristan Wilde" about the author alter ego, employing pen names to good effect, and the life of a Jet City author and columnist. Sure to be a lively and entertaining discussion.

Mixer Roundtable — Writing Media Tie-ins with Christopher Golden & James A. Moore

Christopher Golden and James. A. Moore are talented authors with a large body of original work. However, both have been responsible for writing a number of media tie-in novels for such wildly popular franchises as Alien, Sons of Anarchy, Buffy the Vampire Slayer, and more. In this discussion participants will be able to learn about the process behind obtaining and writing media tie-in novels.

Panels and Workshops (Saturday and Sunday)

All panels, workshops, and readings require a weekend or day pass to attend.

Going it Alone — Independent/Self/Hybrid Publishing Strategies

Thanks to electronic publishing platforms and print on demand, The barrier to entry for publishing is currently at an all time low. Join a group of talented authors and publishers who have cracked the code to quality independent publishing and marketing. *Moderated by Scott Christian Carr.*

Special Guest Panel: State of the Union for Speculative Fiction and Art

An annual tradition. We assemble all of our special guests on one panel to discuss the trends impacting speculative fiction and art over the past year, and in the year to come. This panel serves as our official kick-off and welcome to AnthoCon 2015. *Moderated by Tim Deal.*

Anthologies: Editing/Constructing/Themes

Collections of short fiction still remain one of the most popular mediums for sharing and reading speculative fiction. This panel will explore tips and experiences for enhancing the quality, readability, and marketability of anthologies from the standpoints of authors, editors, and publishers. *Moderated by Holly Newstein.*

Workshop: Gene O'Neill, Autobiography in Fiction

The workshop panel will introduce the concept of the hitchhiking effect, the emotional connection the good writer establishes with the good reader. Some background, some examples, some sensory triggers. With time for audience questions, response, and participation. *Moderated by Gene O'Neill.*

Business Savvy: Understanding Contracts/Preventing Exploitation

Writers and artists are routinely asked to provide their work in exchange for "exposure." In some cases they sign seemingly sound contracts only to see contract terms change at a later time. This panel will help creative workers navigate the complex legal landscape of creative contracts by exposing some of the pitfalls of exploitive agreements. *Moderated by Bracken MacLeod.*

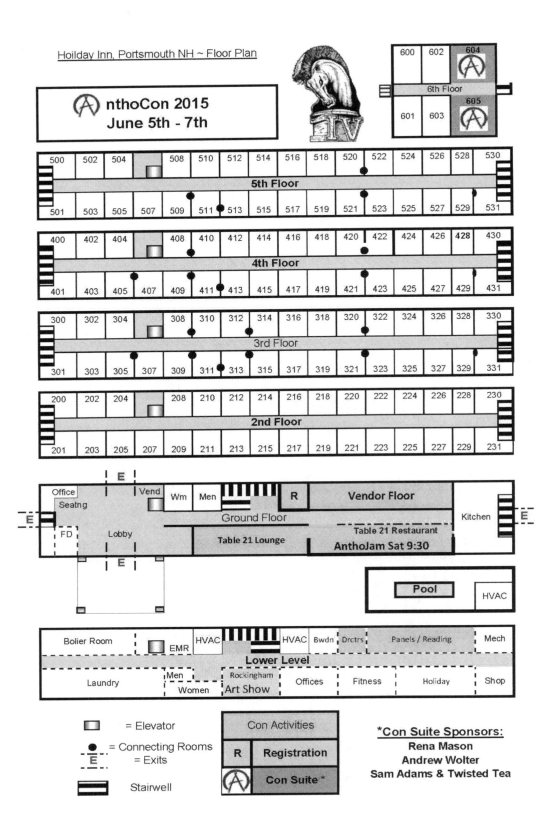

Hoilday Inn, Portsmouth NH ~ Floor Plan

AnthoCon 2015
June 5th - 7th

6th Floor: 600, 602, 604, 601, 603, 605

5th Floor: 500, 502, 504, 508, 510, 512, 514, 516, 518, 520, 522, 524, 526, 528, 530 / 501, 503, 505, 507, 509, 511, 513, 515, 517, 519, 521, 523, 525, 527, 529, 531

4th Floor: 400, 402, 404, 408, 410, 412, 414, 416, 418, 420, 422, 424, 426, 428, 430 / 401, 403, 405, 407, 409, 411, 413, 415, 417, 419, 421, 423, 425, 427, 429, 431

3rd Floor: 300, 302, 304, 308, 310, 312, 314, 316, 318, 320, 322, 324, 326, 328, 330 / 301, 303, 305, 307, 309, 311, 313, 315, 317, 319, 321, 323, 325, 327, 329, 331

2nd Floor: 200, 202, 204, 208, 210, 212, 214, 216, 218, 220, 222, 224, 226, 228, 230 / 201, 203, 205, 207, 209, 211, 213, 215, 217, 219, 221, 223, 225, 227, 229, 231

Ground Floor: Office, Seatng, FD, Lobby, Vend, Wm, Men, R, Vendor Floor, Kitchen, Table 21 Lounge, Table 21 Restaurant, AnthoJam Sat 9:30

Pool, HVAC

Lower Level: Bolier Room, EMR, HVAC, HVAC, Bwdn, Drctrs, Panels / Reading, Mech, Laundry, Men, Women, Rockingham Art Show, Offices, Fitness, Holiday, Shop

= Elevator
= Connecting Rooms
E = Exits
Stairwell

Con Activities
R — Registration
Con Suite *

*Con Suite Sponsors:
Rena Mason
Andrew Wolter
Sam Adams & Twisted Tea

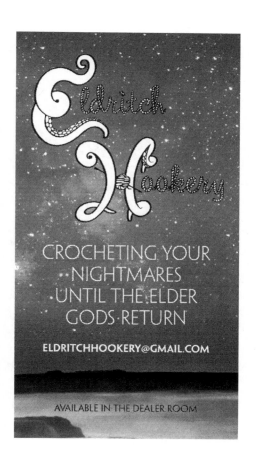
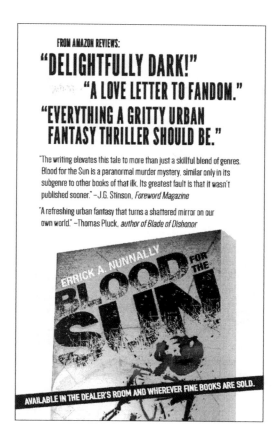

Special Guests

CHRISTOPHER GOLDEN is the award-winning, best-selling author of such novels as The Myth Hunters, Wildwood Road, The Boys Are Back in Town, The Ferryman, Strangewood, Of Saints and Shadows, and (with Tim Lebbon) The Map of Moments. He has also written books for teens and young adults, including Poison Ink, Soulless, and the thriller series Body of Evidence, honored by the New York Public Library and chosen as one of YALSA's Best Books for Young Readers. Upcoming teen novels include a new series of hardcover YA fantasy novels co-authored with Tim Lebbon and entitled The Secret Journeys of Jack London.

TOM MONTELEONE: Of his forty books, his NY Times bestselling novel, The Blood of the Lamb received the 1993 Bram Stoker Award, and The New York Times Notable Book of the Year Award. Tom Monteleone has been a professional writer

since 1972. He has published more than 100 short stories in numerous magazines and anthologies. His notorious column of opinion and entertainment, The Mothers And Fathers Italian Association, currently appears in Cemetery Dance magazine. He is the editor of seven anthologies, including the highly acclaimed Borderlands series edited with his wife, Elizabeth, of which, Borderlands 5, won a Bram Stoker Award. He has been an Instructor at the

JAMES A. MOORE is the author of over twenty novels, including the critically acclaimed Fireworks, Under The Overtree, Blood Red, Blood Harvest, the Serenity Falls trilogy (featuring his recurring anti-hero, Jonathan Crowley) Cherry Hill and his most recent novels Smile No More and the forthcoming Blind Shadows (co-authored with Charles R. Rutledge). He has twice been nominated for the Bram Stoker Award and spent three years as an officer in the Horror Writers Association, first as Secretary and later as Vice President.

Never one to stay in one genre for too long, James has recently written two Young Adult Novels, Subject Seven and the sequel Run. He is working on the third book in the series, tentatively called The Hornet's Nest. Just to keep things properly muddied, he is also working ion an epic sword and sorcery trilogy, a young adult end of the world series and a modern day steampunk series. Why be normal?

Being a confirmed Luddite, he is working up the nerve to plunge completely into the electronic publications age.

Soon to be published is his first non-fiction book, DINNER FOR ONE, being an examination of life after the loss of his wife of twenty years.

HOLLY NEWSTEIN'S short fiction has appeared in Cemetery Dance Magazine and the anthologies BORDERLANDS 5, THE NEW DEAD, IN LAYMON'S TERMS, EPITAPHS: THE JOURNAL OF THE NEW ENGLAND HORROR WRITERS ASSOCIATION, EVIL JESTER DIGEST VOL. 2, and HAUNTED MAINE. Her collaboration with Rick Hautala, "Trapper Boy" appeared in DARK DUETS, an anthology edited by Christopher Golden, published by Harper Voyager in January 2014. Her story "Eight Minutes" was part of ANTHOLOGY II, published October 2013 from The Four Horsemen Press. She was the featured author in the July 2014 edition of LampLight Magazine, with her story "Shadows and Light."

She is also the coauthor of the novels ASHES and THE EPICURE with Ralph W. Bieber, published originally under the pen name H.R.Howland. She lives in Maine with her dogs, Keira and Remy.

GENE O'NEILL has seen 150 of his short stories and novellas published. Some of these have been assembled in four collections. He has published five novels, with two to be published, THE CONFESSIONS OF ST. ZACH in the four book set, THE CAL WILD CHRONICLES, from Thunderstorm Books. THE WHITE PLAGUE is being shopped by his agent. He's been a Stoker finalist nine times, bringing home two haunted house for his collection, TASTE OF TENDERLOIN and for Long Fiction for THE BLUE HERON. He writes full time now, busy on a pair of promised novellas.

SUSAN SCOFIELD is an artist currently based in York, PA. She studied Visual Arts at the University of California San Diego, earning a Bachelor of Arts Degree with an emphasis in Photography. Although versed in many mediums, Susan focuses primarily on photography and assemblage. Her work explores themes of details overlooked, the blatantly present but often unseen.

Susan has appeared three times as an exhibiting artist at the AnthoCon Speculative Fiction Convention in New Hampshire, through which she had photographs published in "Anthology: Year Two: Inner Demons Out" and won a Hiram Award. She is a former winner of the "Award of Distinction" at the annual YorkFest celebration in York, PA.

In 2014, she was again selected for the 2014 YorkFest Juried Exhibition, appeared in FLY Magazine, and one of her photographs was chosen for the book cover of "Unfit For Burial" by Wesley Southard.

She is very active in supporting, promoting and participating in the efforts of artists, writers & musicians within York's local creative community and beyond. In late 2013, Susan became co-owner / co-curator of HIVE artspace – a gallery space and arts collective in York, PA.

In Memorium: Tracie Orsi

On February 1, 2015, the world lost one of its most brilliant lights: Tracie Godier Orsi.

Tracie was many things. She was kind and sweet. Sassy and sharp. Caring and gentle. Loud and brazen. And she was fun. Really, really fun.

Tracie owned a successful restaurant and was a published author multiple times over. She loved her friends and her family. Fiercely, thoroughly. She lit up whatever room she entered. And she was easy to fall in love with. Her smile, her laugh, her wit. All magical. But the most magical part of her was her empathy. She listened with purpose. She processed your pain, your joy, your fear—whatever it was—and made it her own. And when she reflected it back on you, she made you feel special. She made you feel like you could conquer the world.

Tracie was a lover. She was a fighter. And she fought and fought all the way to the end. Her time in our community was brief. Way too brief. But her impact on it was huge. Positive and wonderful. And her brilliant light, her beautiful spirit, will not soon be forgotten.

— Meghan Acuri, May 2015

Illustration on facing page by Ogmios

Thanks to Tony Tremblay for his Photos (below)

tracie orsi
author & owner of
ragin' cajun restaurant

2015 Vendor List

Please stop by the Dealer Room and visit our vendors:

Books & Boos

Written Backwards Publishing

Author: Andrew Wolter

Shock Totem Publishing

Author: John M. McIlveen

Author E.j Stevens

New England Horror Writers

Author :M.R. Tighe

Author : Asher Ellis

Author MJ Preston

Great Old Ones Publishing

Apokrupha LLC

Firbolg Publishing

Art by Ogmios / Outside the box comics

Author: James Marino

Author:Jeff O'Brien, Riot Forge Studios

Macabre Maine Publishing

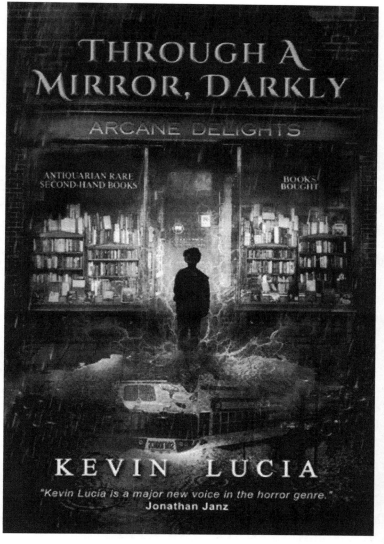

Arcane Delights. Clifton Heights' premier rare and used bookstore. In it, new owner Kevin Ellison has inherited far more than a family legacy, for inside are tales that will amaze, astound, thrill...and terrify.

An ancient evil thirsty for lost souls. A very different kind of taxi service with destinations not on any known map. Three coins that grant the bearer's fondest wish, and a father whose crippling grief gives birth to something dark and hungry.

Every town harbors secrets. Kevin Ellison is about to discover those that lurk in the shadows of Clifton Heights.

Releasing in the Con Suite, Friday night, 9:30 - THROUGH A MIRROR, DARKLY.

Juried Art Show Members

Timoleon Batsaouras is an artist based in Athens, Greece. He studied at the School of Fine Arts of Athens, and is the winner of numerous awards and recognition plaques for his work in the digital art medium. His work explores painting, digital art, photography, comics, graffiti, and video art but his main work includes collages, playing with images to create dreamlike visions, deeply poetic and engaging, with a strong emotional impact.

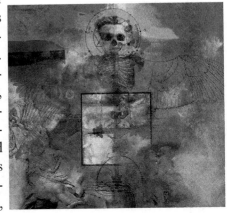

He has previously participated in:
~ affordable art fair Milan ,NIU
~ art space in Poblenou Barcelona
~ ART BODENSEE, Dornbirn - Land Vorarlberg - Austria, <Mass Hypnosis>
~ Devilstone Festival Lithuania,
~ Piazzetta Numero Dure,Cormons Gorizia Italy
~Milwaukee Macabre Dark Art Gala , 6 Wings Studio, Milwaukee, WI
~ HIVE artspace, York, PA
~ His work has been included in bastardmagazine. dc, Bleaq and more.

High-quality photographic prints of his work are available through HIVE artspace in York, Pennsylvania.

While living in California, **Judi Calhoun** majored in Art and English at Palomar College, in San Marcos. Judi studied the pure contour method as well as intensive creative communication discipline under the tutelage of Children's book illustrator, Michael Ster-

nagle and portrait artist Steven Miller. Their substantial training provided Judi with a well-rounded education in both portrait work and illustration.

Many of her Watercolor paintings have graced the covers of Web magazines, such as Pithy Pages for an Erudite Mind, and Dual Coast Magazine to name only a few.

In 2009, Judi was the winner of the Artist Innovation Award by Art Works, NH and twice commissioned to create a cancellation stamp for the US Postal service. You can view Judi's work by visiting her website at, http://judiartist2.wix.com/judisartwork

Barry Lee Dejasu lives in Providence, Rhode Island, with his partner, author Catherine Grant, and two cats. Starting with crayon masterpieces on walls and magnets on TV screens, and working his way up through doodles in the margins of many a notebook, Barry has spent most of his life creating art. Although now primarily an author, his passion for creating art stayed alive and well, and for the past couple of years he's

been designing and creating custom bookmarks, with a particular focus on his favorite genre: horror. It is Barry's great honor to share some of his bookmark art here at Anthocon, with prints available for purchase.

Jan Kozlowski is a freelance writer, editor and researcher who has been crocheting since childhood, but it's only been in the past couple of years that it occurred to her to combine it with her love of the horror genre. She started making stuffed Cthulhus for friends and that obsession with crafting horror-themed fiber art has evolved into her new business venture, Eldritch Hookery.

Please stop by the New England Horror Writers'

booth in the Dealer's Room to check out her crocheted creations and her novel, DIE, YOU BASTARD! DIE!, just reissued by Deadite Press.

Michele Mixell is a photographer, artist, author, dinosaur wrangler, and destroyer of worlds originally from Central PA. She premiered her first solo photography exhibit at the York Emporium in 2014, and is a frequent exhibitor at HIVE artspace in York, PA.

Her work includes a vast range of subjects, from the tiny, unnoticed details of everyday life to darker, more macabre fare. Her focus tends towards the rustic and rusted, the over-grown and over-looked, the lost, the broken and the discarded.

Prints of her work, as well as other artwork and items are available for purchase through her Etsy shop, SavageMouseStudios.

Ogmios is an artist and the publisher for Outside The Box Comics. Art by Ogmios can be found on many published book covers and interior pages as well as his premier anthology comic "Summerlands Fanzine". Ogmios likes to use pencil, ink and digital paint when illustrating and is focused on Myth, Horror, Sci-Fi, and Fantasy. See more from Ogmios and Outside The Box Comics at www.ArtBy-Ogmios.com.

Lisa Reinke has been creating art her whole life. A graduate of Col-orado State University with a Bachelor of Fine Arts Degree and a concentration in Graphic Design, she primarily works in oils, and has been experimenting with digital media and oil pastels. Lisa loves strong visuals, vibrant color, repeated patterns and most recently playing with positive and negative space. She lives and paints in Exeter, NH, and for years she worked with Mark Wholley and jOhnny Morse at Lonza Biologics before leaving biotech to concentrate on her artwork.

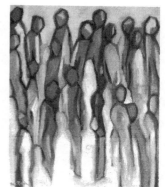

She shares a love for speculative and imaginative narratives in all the genres that AnthoCon celebrates. You can see more of Lisa's artwork at www.lisareinke.com.

Ann Shaver lives near Mt Gretna, PA, and is a self-taught mixed media / mosaic artist. She loves working with the architecture of natural materials, especially bones, and is fascinated with creating new creatures out of ordinary items. She also sells vintage goods (jewelry, buttons, beads, etc.), giving her a rich source of inspiration, as well as an endless supply of playthings.

The chupacabras (there are now 25 in existence) began with a whitetail deer antler mount that her husband brought home from an auction. As the face began to take shape, she began to think of them as chupacabras and that tickled her fancy (her first exposure to the legend of the chupacabra was from an episode of the X-Files that stuck with her after all these years). Each one has his own personality, dictated by the shape of the mount and the materials at hand. The individual names come to Ann as she works. These creatures are heavily influenced by a mixture of tribal and lucha libre masks.

More from **Susan Scofield:**

Works by Susan Scofield
Artist GoH

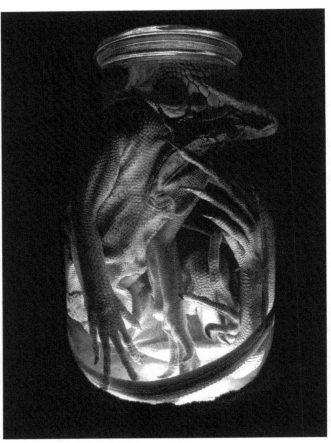

Artist Guest of Honor

Susan Scofield

Susan Scofield is the owner and curator of HIVE artspace Gallery in York, PA. She studied Visual Arts at the University of California San Diego, earning a Bachelor of Arts Degree with an emphasis in photography. Although versed in many mediums, Susan focuses primarily on photography and assemblage. Her work explores themes of details overlooked, things blatantly present but often unseen, as well as visiting the realms of natural history and biology.

Susan is a former winner of YorkFest's "Award of Distinction," has appeared multiple times as a Featured Artist at the Anthocon Speculative Fiction Convention in New Hampshire, and will return in 2015 as their Artist Guest of Honor and curator of the Anthocon Art Exhibition. She has exhibited at YorkArts Gallery, The Parliament, CityArt Gallery, York College Galleries at Marketview Arts, The Yorktowne Hotel, and SevVen Gallery in Huntington Beach, CA.

Participant Biographies

T.G. Arsenault is the author of the novels Forgotten Souls and Bleeding the Vein. His short fiction has appeared online and in multiple anthologies, most recently Anthology Year Two: Inner Demons Out; Canopic Jars: Tales of Mummies and Mummification; and Widowmakers: A Benefit Anthology of Dark Fiction.

Meghan Arcuri is writes fiction and poetry. Her short stories can be found in various anthologies, including Chiral Mad (Written Backwards) and Insidious Assassins (Smart Rhino). She lives with her family in New York's Hudson Valley. Please visit her at meghanarcuri.com or facebook.com/meg.arcuri.

Michael Bailey is the multi-award-winning author of PALINDROME HANNAH, PHOENIX ROSE and PSYCHOTROPIC DRAGON (novels), SCALES AND PETALS and INKBLOTS AND BLOOD SPOTS (short story / poetry collections), and editor of PELLUCID LUNACY, QUALIA NOUS, THE LIBRARY OF THE DEAD, and the CHIRAL MAD anthologies published by Written Backwards. He is also the Managing Editor of Science Fiction for Dark Regions Press.

E. A. Black's horror fiction has appeared in "Teeming Terrors", New England Horror Writers "Wicked Tales 3", "Stupefying Stories", "Zippered Flesh 2: More Tales Of Body Enhancements Gone Bad" and "Mirages: Tales From Authors Of The Macabre" (edited by Trent Zelazny).

Bram Stoker Nominee Hal Bodner is best known for his horror comedy novels, including BITE CLUB. He also writes paranormal romance and comic "caper" thrillers. Most of his work explores gay cultural issues and themes.

Scott Christian Carr has been a radio talk show host, editor of a flying saucer magazine, fishmonger, spelunker, psychonaut, journalist, award winning poet, TV producer, and author. He is a Bram Stoker Award nominee, Scriptapalooza 1st Place Winner for Best Original TV Pilot, and in 1999, he was awarded The Hunter S. Thompson Award for Outstanding Journalism. www.scottchristiancarr.com.

Barry Lee Dejasu is a columnist for the movie blog Cinema Knife Fight, as well as an editor for Shock Totem Publications. He lives in Rhode Island with his lover, author Catherine Grant.

Thom Erb is a genre fiction writer exploring all shades of darkness, light and the varying definitions of heroism and the reluctant hero. Refusing to pigeonhole his writing, Thom crafts tales blurring the lines of horror, fantasy, thriller and beyond. Find more at: www.thomerb.com.

Timothy P. Flynn resides in Haverhill, MA. His previous poetry has been in Space and Time magazine Issue # 115, Anthology: Year One, and Anthology: Year Two: Inner Demons Out. Tim is a husband and father of three, a member of the NEHW(New England Horror Writers), and an online student at SNHU studying Creative Writing/English.

Dan Foley is the author of the novel "Death's Companion", and "The Whispers of Crows, a collection of short stories, both are available through Necon e-books, Amazon and B&N. He has also published in various anthologies and magazines in the U.S. Canada, England and Australia. Find him at www.deathscompanion.com.

Doungjai gam , a native of Thailand, now resides in Connecticut with her family. She is a seven-time Necon E-Books Flash Fiction winner and has been published in LampLight Magazine. Find her on Facebook at www.facebook.com/djai76.

Larissa Glasser (larissaglasser.com) is an academic librarian from Boston. She has published nonfiction in Harvard Review, The Boston Phoenix, and Maelstrom. Her fiction debut appears in The Healing Monsters anthology (Despumation Press).

Scott T. Goudsward is a New England writer. He is one of the coordinators of the New England Horror Writers. New in the writing world, Scott has a non-fiction book co-written with his brother David, "Horror Guide to Massachusetts," an anthology co-edited with Rachel Kenley, "Once Upon an Apocalypse." His short fiction has most recently appeared in "Atomic Age Cthulhu," "Wicked Seasons," "Dark Rites of Cthulhu" and "Bugs!" Readers can learn more at www.goudsward.com/scott.

Jacob Haddon is an engineer by day, editor by night and a Viking in his sleep. He can be found online at jacobhaddon.com.

Marianne Halbert's stories have been published by Coach's Midnight Diner, Midnight Screaming, Pill Hill Press, Necrotic Tissue Magazine, Blue River Press, ThugLit, Wicked East Press, Evil Jester Press, Static Movement, The Four Horsemen, Grinning Skull Press, Mystery & Horror LLC, Great Old Ones Publishing, Mocha Memoirs Press and more, as well as forthcoming stories with Screaming Spires Press and Evil Jester Comics.

April Hawks writes from a small town in Maine. She has been published by Great Old Ones Publishing and Perpetual Motion Machine Publishers, among others. She is writing a novel.

Laura J. Hickman started writing as a child and had numerous short stories published by Necon ebooks, Six Sentences, and Angelic Knight Press. She would like to thank her friends and family for all their support in her writing.

Patrick Lacey is a horror author from Massachusetts. Follow him on Twitter (@patlacey), find him on Facebook, or visit his website at patrickclacey.wordpress.com.

Esther M. Leiper-Estabrooks has published since college; wrote a column in Writers' Journal for thirty years, and has sold fiction, poetry, and essays in various genres ever since. Most recently, she has appeared in Canopic Jars and Cellar Door.

Bracken MacLeod's stories have appeared in Shroud, Splatterpunk, and Shock Totem. He is the author of MOUNTAIN HOME and WHITE KNIGHT. His next novel, STRANDED, is coming soon from TOR books.

James I. Marino worked in the Marketing Department of a Fortune 500 financial company for eight years before attaining a Master of Fine Arts Degree in Fiction Writing from Southern New Hampshire University and joining the English Department there as an adjunct professor. James has a deep appreciation of nature that can be seen in the well-crafted images that punctuate his writing. He lives on Havenhill Farm in New Hampshire with his wife Megan, their son Max, and several furry friends.

Chris Marrs lives on the west coast of British Columbia. She has a story in A Darke Phantastique, Cycatrix Press, in The Library of the Dead, Written Backwards, and in Dark Discoveries Magazine Issue #25/Femme Fatale. In October 2014 Bad Moon Books published her novella, Everything Leads Back to Alice. Upcoming soon is her novella, Wildwoman, to be released in the Double Down series from JournalStone.

John McIlveen is the author of INFLICTIONS and JERKS. His novel HANNAH WHERE is due in July from Crossroads Press. He works at MIT and lives in Haverhill, MA. Yay tequila!

Michele Mixell is an author, photographer, artist, & dinosaur wrangler from Central Pennsylvania. Her short fiction has appeared in Apokrupha's LampLight Magazine and Dark Bits. Her novella "End of the Night" can be found in their collection FOUR SLEEPLESS NIGHTS.

Gregory L. Norris is a full-time professional writer with numerous publication credits to his resume, mostly in national magazines and fiction anthologies. A former writer at Sci Fi, the official magazine of the Sci Fi Channel, he once worked as a screenwriter on two episodes of Paramount's modern classic, Star Trek: Voyager.

David North-Martino (http://davidnorthmartino.com) is the author of WOLVES OF VENGEANCE. His short stories have appeared in numerous fiction venues including: Epitaphs, Wicked Tales, Anthology: Year Two, and Daughters of Icarus.

Errick Nunnally: raised in Boston, served in the Marine Corps, and graduated from art school. Blood For The Sun is his first published novel along with several short stories in anthologies.

Monica J. O'Rourke has published more than 100 stories in magazines and anthologies, as well as Poisoning Eros, Suffer the Flesh, What Happens in the Darkness, and In the End, Only Darkness.

Craig D.B. Patton writes in a 200-year old manse in Connecticut. His tales are in Anthology: Year Two - Inner Demons Out, Supernatural Tales, Illumen, and other markets. Learn more at flawedcreations.wordpress.com. Follow him on Twitter at @craigdbpatton.

Philip C. Perron is a resident of New Hampshire. You can find his story, Indian Summer, in the anthology, Chiral Mad 2, by Written Backwards Press.

The mind of D.B. Poirier is skewed, slightly, from the foundation of reality. He spends most of his time daydreaming about worlds and place most people are unaware of. A problem he intends to rectify through his writing. www.dbpoirier.com.

Kristi Petersen Schoonover's novel, Bad Apple, is a Pushcart Prize nominee; her short fiction has appeared in several publications. She's received three Norman Mailer Writers Colony Residencies and is an editor for Read Short Fiction.

A native of Salem, Massachusetts, Rob Smales enjoys writing ghost stories, one of which was nominated for a Pushcart Prize in 2012. His first book, Dead of Winter, was named a Superior Achievement in Dark Fiction by Firbolg Publishing's Gothic Library.

E.J. Stevens is the author of fourteen works of speculative fiction, including the SPIRIT GUIDE series, the HUNTERS' GUILD series, and the award-winning IVY GRANGER urban fantasy series.

T.T. Zuma has had numerous horror and noir stories published in various print anthologies, magazines, and websites. Zuma also write reviews of dark fiction and horror novels for Horror World and Cemetery Dance magazine. He lives in New Hampshire with his wife, Paula.

From Above

By Mark Wholley and Richard Wright

Grey morning light smogged through the small window and into the red kitchen, where it found Glyn sitting on a burgundy faux leather stool at the breakfast bar. His hands wrapped around a coffee mug, and he stared at the rising steam. The mug was too hot to clasp, but he did so anyway because the pain that pulsed through his hands made him feel connected to something.

The other person in the room, sitting on the far side of the counter, wasn't really there. The absence was not her fault, but he resented her for it anyway. He missed sitting with her each morning, sharing gossip, examining the world, even though they had never done those things. Dawn had always brought with it the rush of snatched breakfasts, fast showers, and the countdown to work. There had been no time to talk.

It was the possibility that he missed, the chance that something would change and such a moment of bonding would transpire. That was her role. She was the one that people told things to, and invited places. Glyn was her leech, draining away experience and news like hot blood. He bathed in her crimson reports.

Now that she was dead, the world had cut him loose. That was what it felt like. He was no longer invited.

A shuffle and squawk drew his attention to the window. Five pigeons were lined up on the sill, feathers puffed and heads drawn down. He frowned. They were frequent visitors, because the ledge was in the lee of the building and offered protection from the frequent driving rains. Today though, the weather was clear. He got up, crossing the kitchen to the window, and craned his neck to look at the sky. All was chrome stillness.

The pigeons ignored him, even when he tapped the glass.

***

The train into the city centre was full, but quiet. Nobody chatted. Telephones did not ring. There was not even the black and white swish of newspaper pages being turned.

On an ordinary day Glyn would have been a paper swisher, but the strange stillness in the carriage forbade him his usual routine. It would make him stand out, mark him as different. Being looked at, no matter what the reason, desiccated him from the inside.

Instead he stared straight ahead, trying to watch everybody else from the corner of his eye. Nobody paid any attention to him. Instead, they looked out of the window. Out, and up.

***

At the grand arch of the station entrance a small crowd of suits had gathered, blocking the way. They muttered to one another, and occasionally looked up at the sky. Glyn looked too, but there was nothing to see. He turned to a young woman with a severe ponytail. "Excuse me? Is there something up there?"

She did not want to take her eyes off the cold, flat sky, but the question was clearly so astonishing that she forced herself. For a moment she stared at him, making him want to dissolve on the spot so that he could drain safely along the gutter, escaping into the sewers in a hot gush. Understanding spread across her face, ironing out the creases of dismay in her forehead. She shook her head, a little sad, and returned her gaze to the heavens. "Nothing important." Her voice was made of afterthoughts. "Nothing you need to concern yourself with."

***

As was his custom, he wore headphones in work. The pale wire trailed into his pocket, but there was no device there to plug it into. The headphones allowed him to pretend that it was his choice not to speak to anybody in the office, but he wanted always to be sure that if somebody did try to bridge the gulf he could hear them and respond. He lived in fear of such a moment, at the same time as he prayed for it every morning.

The day's data was piled next to him, a numerical sludge he didn't understand and needed only to type into his keyboard accurately. It swallowed him for a couple of hours before he realised that there was no noise. Nobody had walked past his cubicle. Nobody was speaking on the phone or shouting over to a friend. It was silent.

He took the headphones out, feeling instantly naked, and stood.

On the far side of the office all was normal. Colleagues who could not remember his name sat in their little rectangles and battered their drab keyboards. With the headphones out, he could hear the little noise that drifted across the large open plan room. Nearer to him, the desks were empty. Everybody on his own team was stood by the exit, around the water cooler. Jerry was speaking quickly in a low voice, and the others were nodding along with him. Every now and again somebody cast a fast and anxious look at the window.

They were on the fourth floor, and had a view of the office block across the road.

Glyn seized his chance, and scurried across to join them. Whether it was too overt and they saw him coming, or whether the meeting came to a natural end, they turned and walked past him to their desks, leaving him stranded. Jerry nodded as he passed, but it was an absent gesture born of courteous instinct more than familiarity.

So that he did not look foolish standing there, he grabbed a paper cup and held it under the cooler tap. There was a gurgle, but nothing came out. They had emptied it. He pretended to drink anyway, so that they would not see his discomfort and laugh.

***

Instead of leaving the building and having his limp sandwiches in the park, Glyn made his way to the staff canteen with a red dread about his heart. Hav-

ing a strategy was all very well, but he had always been more thinker than doer. The plan was simple enough though, with a low chance of either failure or embarrassment. While he might be unwelcome among any given group of colleagues, he would take his tray to a table near to the largest gathering there and listen in. They might clam up when he approached, but after a few moments he would become invisible to them again and they would start to talk. Practical invisibility was his gift.

Outside the doors of the canteen, he paused and adjusted himself. Tie straight, shirt tucked in, zipper pulled up. Nothing to see here.

A gentle push of the swinging doors, and he stepped through. Nobody gave him a second glance, because nobody was there. The room was empty. The company employed over five hundred people, and none of them were hungry. Even the servers were absent. The metal trays were full of food, some still steaming, but there was nobody behind the counter.

Glyn walked towards the pile of wooden trays at the end of the service area, and rested his fingertips on one while he craned his neck to scan the kitchen. It was abandoned too. Nobody jumped out to say boo.

Taking a seat at one of the tables, he pulled out his phone and opened Twitter. A slide of his thumb took him to what would normally be a list of worldwide trending topics, but today there was only one.

#fromabove

The hashtag did something to his throat that made it tiny, like a reed. Air whistled in and out like steam evacuating a kettle. When he found the courage to press his thumb to the hashtag and bring up all the tweets that used it, his screen went blank. No posts. He opened a tweet of his own, and wrote:

What is happening?

He waited. Nobody retweeted. Nobody replied. Nobody acknowledged him at all.

***

When he returned to the office, nobody was there either. After a guilty glance around to confirm that he really was alone, he stepped into the cubicle along from his. Jenna had left her screen unlocked, and there was an email open. The subject read: ALL STAFF TAKE NOTE. The message itself was an invitation to a meeting on the second floor, immediately after lunch. The email had been sent two hours previously.

Returning to his own cubicle, he unlocked his screen and checked his own email. Nothing. He had not been copied in.

***

Although he did not have the courage to walk into a roomful of people who did not want him there, he did check the conference lounge before he left the building. The doors were closed, and when he gave the handle the gentlest of twists he found that they were locked. A murmur misted through the doors, but no matter how hard he strained he could not hear the words.

So he abandoned ship. There was nobody in the elevator. Nobody was standing around in the lobby. The security guard at the main entrance was elsewhere.

At least there were people on the street, scurrying with their heads down, pausing only to glance at the blank slate sky. When he arrived at the subway there was a tattered old man standing on a wooden stool beside the steps. A small group had gathered to hear him speak, but by the time Glyn was in earshot it was over. The group dispersed, and the old man made a poor show of finding something interesting to look at further down the street. Glyn strode by as though he did not care, and caught a glimpse of the

single word scrawled on the brown cardboard sign the silent prophet still clasped.

SOON

***

The train was packed with silent travellers, but the seat beside Glyn remained empty. An elderly lady wobbled in the aisle next to it, her discomfort obvious. On a different day he would have made eye contact, perhaps even gestured for her to sit, but now he did not dare. She would refuse as politely as she could, and everybody would hear, and they would know that he knew that they knew that he didn't know.

It was safer to stay silent and pretend.

When he disembarked and took the stairs back to the street, rats bounded past him, along the edge of the wall, heading up. Nobody else looked surprised, so he tried to fake nonchalance too.

The cemetery was a fifteen-minute walk, and he spent most of it looking at his feet.

***

The stone angel stared at him as he approached the grave, grasping the crucifix headstone as though some powerful storm might rip it away. Glyn nodded a polite hello as always. The angel had intense eyes, and it seemed rude not to acknowledge it.

He walked past, to the next grave along. This headstone was a simple white slab, with metallic lettering spelling out her name and a date eight months before. It might have been marble, the slab, but nobody had consulted him and so he could not be sure it was the genuine article. He was lucky that they had remembered to invite him to the funeral at all.

"I hate you now," he told that uncertain headstone. "They would have told you. You would have told me. I would have been part of it with you."

Did he hate her? Or everybody else? He wasn't sure. He knew that he was scared, and alone. Beyond that hot mess of dread, he wasn't sure of anything at all.

A mutter made him turn his head. Further along the row an older couple stood over another crooked cross. They weren't looking at the grave, nor were they scanning the sky. Instead they were watching a copse of trees beyond the cemetery wall, speaking to one another with animated resignation. Glyn tracked across and saw what had made their hearts so heavy. Birds were flying out of the tree, one at a time. A pigeon flew, and then a sparrow. A starling followed, then another pigeon. That they were making so organised an exit was less startling than their direction of travel.

They flew straight up, hard and fast, like feathered hailstones in reverse. Other trees were releasing their own silent, winged processions.

Glyn's heart fluttered. He turned to leave, then stopped. The angel that was always there to meet his eyes and accept his greeting had tilted back its head and was looking up. Its expression had not changed, but there was a new composure there that he had never noted before.

betrayal cut him, and he started to cry. Then he ran onto the street, dodging strangers who tutted as they watched the skies.

***

He got home, exhausted and shaking, he locked his door behind him and closed the curtains. After a few moments respite in the chair she had once chosen for him, he unplugged his telephone, and the television, and the ancient desktop computer he had meant to replace.

Then he wept and waited.

When it finally descended, he met it untethered and alone.

"...It was safer to stay silent and pretend..."

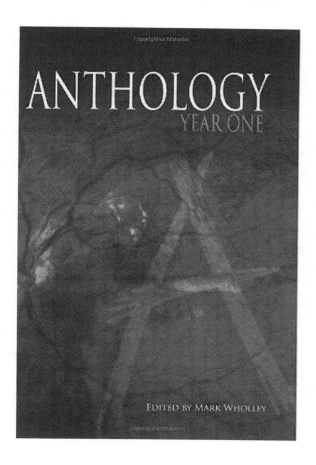

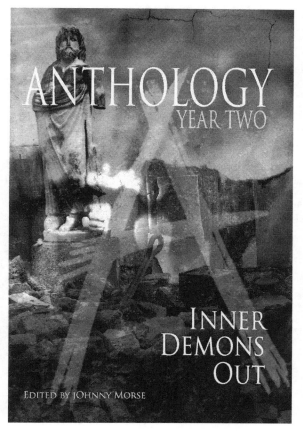

Richard Wright and "The 52."

The three stories presented in this programme (and thank you to the Wholley Horseman for asking whether they could be included) come from a project called 'The 52'. It started as a means to get out of my own head and into other peoples. Readers - or anybody who saw the posts about it and wanted to play - were invited to send me a photograph or piece of at, around which I would construct a story. So far phase 1 of the project is complete, and twelve such stories and images can be found on my website to be read for free. As you read this at Anthocon, phase 2 is about to begin. Images exist, and soon stories will too. I hope you'll pop by and see how the whole thing is going.

"... a means to get out of my own head..."

These three stories could not exist without the things that Mark Wholley, Susan Scofield, and Jackie Blewett saw and sent me. Thanks to all three, and to the other contributors past and future, for joining in.

Richard Wright lives in Scotland and makes strange, dark fictions. Some he keeps caged at www. richardwright.org. Others he seals in bytes and paper, such as his historical tale of obsessions and murder 'The Flesh Market'. Devour these tales, before they devour you.

I Am Hope

by Jackie Blewett and Richard Wright

There wasn't much of the world left. You could see it all from the room at the top of the lift shaft that climbed the side of the cliff on rickety struts of dull green iron. The rock face receded at the top, and so a narrow enclosed walkway ran from the shaft to terra firma. From the room above the shaft, where rusted the gears and motors had once hauled up the fragile carriage, the woman looked down on the walkway's tented roof of corrugated iron as it vanished back into the sodden fog. It had been several weeks since she had been able to see the end of the walkway, and she could not say for certain whether it still led anywhere she wanted to go.

There was more to see on the other side of the lift shaft, bland though it was. In the distance on the left she could still make out the tip of a headland, and the crumble of ancient castle that perched there. The sea far below was a dull grey that blurred into the pervasive mists, but sometimes she could make out the white crests of occasional waves. The room's windows were smeared on the outside with brown dirt. She was not brave enough to climb out and wipe them clean, so when she stared at the headland, wondering whether anybody was trapped there, she saw it in sepia, like an ancient photograph. Soon she would be unable to see anything at all. The grey would gather close and claim her, as it had her family. The children went first, long before she had fled for the heights.
Swallowed. Gone.

Clive went later, one afternoon before the fog had claimed the cliff top. They had picnicked there, nibbling ham from a tin and drinking bottled water, watching the wispy edge of the encroaching void. It was a slow advance, not one you could see with the naked eye. To the observer the fog looked solid and still, until one morning you woke and realised that something that had been there was now gone.

Like Clive. There one moment, staring out to see with mournful eyes. Gone the next. She had glanced away for second, and he had left her. Survival had owned only half of his heart. The children owned the rest, and it was inevitable that one day he would race into the grey to see if they were there.

It was a compulsion she resisted. Perhaps one day she would stand at the edge of that corrugated roof, take a deep breath, and throw herself into the warm bank of fog that was making its slow way up the cliff face – but not yet. For reasons she could not explain, she waited out each day. The water and food supplies they had brought with them, piled in a corner in the small room at the top of the shaft, would not last much longer.

Each night she shivered beneath a tarpaulin, listening to the shuffling of the lone seagull perched on the roof. It was the only living thing she had seen for weeks, and would be dead if she had not shared her rations with it. Sometimes it took flight towards the fog, over the waters, as though it had forgotten the danger. Her heart pounded each time, for she could not bear to be the only living thing left in the world. It had always banked away before it entered. Somehow, deep within its avian brain, it knew there was no coming back.

Perhaps she had an avian brain too, else she would follow Clive and the children. They were probably waiting for her, one way or another, but she could not yet abandon her little sliver of world. It was important that somebody remain, in case the lost came looking.

***

Hope appeared from nowhere one day, as she sat at the door above the ladder down to the walkway, dangling her feet and scooping tuna from a tin with her fingers. The fish smell was rich and pure, connecting her to the ocean that she could hear but no longer see. The water had been swallowed, along with the distant headland, six sleeps ago. Below there was only a fluffy bed of ominous cloud.

At first she did not know what the itch at the back of her brain was. She chewed and swallowed, staring at the perfect blank of the grey below, allowing it into her mind so that she did not have to think sad thoughts. Her emptiness was shattered by her own voice, echoing around her head. Look, she shouted at herself. A thing! A difference! Turn your head and look!

It was a shape in the fog that had caught her

eye, at the point where it swallowed the roof of the walkway. Not just a shape, but a man-shape. She wanted very much for it to be Clive, but as soon as she focussed she knew it was too tall. Whoever it was sat cross-legged, but his back was long and his shoulders slender. There was a suggestion of long hair, and she did not know why she was so certain that the ephemeral figure was male.

She did not know how many sleeps had passed since she had last seen another person. For a time after Clive disappeared she had counted them, but eventually the number had grown meaningless. Lots. Lots of lonely sleeps.

Now there was a person, and she was terrified. Every beat of her heart was a paralysing death, pinning her in place and killing her over and over. She did not want that shape to be a person, not really. There was contentment to be had in drifting towards extinction. If that was a person, sitting perfectly still and crosslegged past the boundary between the world and whatever was eating it, then she had to wake up and do things. Something surged in her, a tickling electricity that both weakened her limbs and made it impossible to sit still. Her mind lit up with dreams and possibilities.

After so much stillness it was too much. She burst into snuffling tears, pulled her legs up, and scuttled to the far side of the motors in the centre of the room. She sat there for a while, rocking and crying with her knees drawn to her chest, hidden by rusting metal teeth. By the time she had allowed herself the possibility that she might not be mad, and there might be another person in the world, he no longer was.

**

That night her seagull left. Scrabbling at the roof, disturbing her dead slumber, it found purchase and took off. Coming wide awake, she leaped to her feet and stumbled to the window, pressing her face to the filthy glass as she scanned the monotony. Although it was dark, her gull's movement against the bleakness drew her eyes as it soared away. She could not see the line of the fog wall, but the bird moved with such sure intent that she assumed it lost even while she tracked it.

At what must surely have been the last pos-

sible moment it banked, down and to the left, then back towards her. She allowed herself to breathe, but only until she realised it was coming no closer. For an aching moment, it held in the air, wings working furiously, and then it was drawn back. The fog had grown impatient. She beat a weak hand on the glass as it flew backwards and vanished.

Sliding down the wall, flattened by grief, she sobbed and rocked and waited for the dawn.

**

The man in the fog returned to her the following afternoon, and she did not allow herself to hesitate. Snatching up her last bag of salt and vinegar crisps, she scurried down the ladder and onto the corrugated iron. In her haste she slipped on the slick, uneven surface, and for a moment believed that she would tumble out into the void whether she wanted to or not. With a mighty effort, she stiffened and regained her balance.

Her visitor was kneeling, his hands in his lap, his head tilted in overt curiosity. As she stumbled towards him she realised he was naked. Fog somehow clung to his skin, clothing him in nothing at all. He was bald now, and young, and even behind the edge of the fog she saw that his flesh was alabaster and his eyes alive with things she had forgotten how to feel.

Swallowed by the rush, she almost stepped into the fog. Only a tiny twitch of his lips brought her out of herself in time. There was a solid edge to the murk that the pea soupers of her childhood had never shown, and her nose was almost pressed to it. Drawing in a shuddering breath, she stepped back.

"Hello," he said.

When she tried to reply she found her throat weak from silence, and was only able to croak a vague greeting. While she swallowed, trying to moisten her mouth, she held up her bag of crisps like a sacrificial offering. He shook his head, wisps of vapour floating out from him in the shape of his head, like ripples in a pond.

"You're alone here," he told her. She nodded. "But you stay?"

She nodded again, and made her mouth work through force of will. "Who are you?"

"I am Hope." His voice was mellow and sweet, filled with all the people she loved.

"I… is that your name?"

"It is what I am."

A fierce anger turned her lips to a snarl that she wished she could wipe away. "I don't have hope anymore."

"So why do you stay?"

"I'm afraid."

He snorted, and fog blew from his nose like cigarette smoke. She craved cigarettes more than she had ever imagined she could. "No. It would be easy to go. It would end things. You choose not to, every day, because you hope."

"I miss them so much."

"You want them back. You hope."

She let her head hang, embarrassed to have the futility of it put to words. "Yes."

"I sensed you. The last hope in this world. I had to see for myself."

"Is Hope your name?"

"It is what I am."

"Hope." The word filled her mouth, and when she swallowed it blossomed in her heart. "If you're here…" He nodded, and Clive's scent fell over her, the faded morning aroma of after-shave and sweat. She could feel the weight of a child on her back, arms around her neck as a he rode the pony with shrill cries of terror and delight. Music filled her head, the violins and cellos she had listened to while pregnant, so that the person growing inside her might be soothed.

Precious though they were, the phantoms overwhelmed her and she dropped to her knees

with a clang. The shudder of the metal banished the crush of memories.

"A little gift," Hope told her. "You have waited a long time, and it makes me glad that you hold me so close. Tomorrow I must return, and make hopes manifest."

"Manifest? Real? You'll make hopes real?"

"That's right," he said. "I will."

***

That night, when at last she fell asleep, she dreamed of faces that had been locked deep in her subconscious. They had been dangerous faces, of love and longing, sealed away in sanity's last effort to remain intact. Let free, each was a sparkle in her soul. She woke warmer than she could remember ever being, with a soft smile on her face.

A glance through dirty glass showed that the fog was pressed close now, but her new vitality stole its power to drain her. If it could think, as she had often believed it must, then she hoped it knew that she had won.

For the first time in months she worried about her appearance. She had not washed since she lost access to the sea far below. Dampening a rag on the condensation that had formed on the metal roof, she wiped her face as best she could without a mirror. Her skin tingled when she was done. There was nothing she could do for her once soft and tawney hair, so she tied it back. It was her face that they would fix on, and she wanted their eyes to light up when they recognised her.

She ate double her usual rations for breakfast, and would have taken more if her stomach had not complained at the unaccustomed burden.

Bidding farewell to her little room at the top of the lift shaft, she climbed back down to the corrugated iron roof. Reigning in her eagerness, she walked with exaggerated care to the fog wall, mindful of her near disaster the previous day. It would be beyond ludicrous to slide off after so long clinging to life, especially with the end in sight.

Hope was waiting for her, and he was frowning. "You have done a thing to your face," he pointed out.

Blushing, she raised a hand to her cheek as though she could hide her vanity. "I wanted to feel a bit human. A bit more myself."

His frown deepened. "Why?"

There was something of scorn in his voice, and her heart began to pound. "So that they recognise me. It's been… it's been a while."

With a soft sigh, he closed his eyes and shook his head. It was a sad shake, that she wanted to unsee but could not. "I understand."

"No," she said, as though she could halt the shift in her expectations with a word.

"I am Hope incarnate. I have the power to change the world. These are true things, but you have also misunderstood."

It was impossible to stare him in the face, to impose her will on his, because the fog billowed between them. "You gave me a taste. A child's weight. A lover's scent. Laughter."

"A gift, for holding me close for so long."

"They're what I hope for. There's nothing else."

The fog cleared for a moment, and he could see the dancing shapes behind his hollow eyes. Pain and madness. Death and void. "I am Hope," he told her one last time, "but I am not yours."

Her mouth opened, and she had a moment of clear understanding. Madmen and tyrants had hopes too. Hate could dream with just as much fervour as love.

The fog billowed out from him, blowing past and through her, and she was gone.

The Day She Died

by Susan Scofield and Richard Wright

The cottage was pretty, behatted in thatch and draped in heavy robes of vibrant creeping ivy. The mat at the door told him in crisp black lettering that he was welcome, and everything about the isolated little home cried out that this was true. Even the solitary ceramic gnome, peeking from the spray of bright flowers bordering the path to the door, seemed pleased to see him.

The sun was falling, casting golden light and shadows all around. It was much later in the day than he had planned to arrive, but a puncture on the winding roads between the cottage and the nearest town had been the cause of unplanned delays. He was not a man of practical application, and had waited with fading patience for the arrival of the man in the van who can. The man who could did, in less than ten minutes, leaving him with a gnawing sense of inadequacy.

There was no further time to waste, not if he wanted to get back to his hotel in time to enjoy his evening. He brushed down the front of his suit, checked the shine on his shoes, and placed his briefcase on the mat beside his feet. When he was certain that he had aligned it to a crisp and perfect ninety-degree angle from the door, he knocked once. As he drew his hand back, the door opened and the woman beamed up at him. She must have heard him approach, and been waiting behind the wood for him to announce himself. He did not like that at all. It was disconcerting.

Hiding his annoyance, he gave a thin smile. "Good afternoon. I believe you're expecting me? My apologies for the late hour, but I had a little trouble on the…"

Her eyes were a remarkable green, like the shallows of a tropical sea awaiting a storm. The observation stunned him, because he had never seen a tropical sea. It was one of many things on a bucket list that he knew he would never begin to work through. She wore her blonde hair in pigtails, and her unrestrained smile showed shining white teeth. To his disappointment she did not appear to be insane.

That was going to make his job a little more difficult. Although his assessment was supposed to be objective and unbiased, he knew there was a considerable bonus to be had if he found this woman to be a danger to herself or others. Somebody somewhere wanted her out of this picturesque little property, and he had his eye on a new coffee machine for his kitchen that the extra funds would more than cover. He enjoyed coffee a great deal.

"I've never seen a tropical sea," he said, even though he had intended to properly introduce himself.

"No," said the woman. "That's because you haven't been born yet." It was exactly the sort of statement that would help his case, but in light of his own unusual opening gambit he wasn't certain he could make much use of it. Going forward he would ensure he said only bland and neutral things, so that he could not be later accused of leading her responses.

The woman took his hand in her soft, warm fingers. It was a contact he would have recoiled from on any other day, but as she led him into the hallway he found himself enjoying the sensation. Heat and excitement boiled through him. His briefcase remained on the welcome mat, but he wanted to follow her more than he wanted to retrieve it.

Framed black and white photographs hung on the wall of the narrow hallway, none of them entirely straight. One was of a little girl with tears cascading down her cheeks, sitting alone on a bed in a dark room, lit only by the light falling through a crack in the door.

A second showed the palm of a hand, callused and slightly cupped, and it was impossible to tell whether it was moving to strike the camera or held to conceal something from its lens. The detail astonished him, for he could see the frayed edges of the tiny micro-creases in the skin.

Another showed a dog on the road, lying on its side with its eyes closed. While there were no injuries apparent, its position beside the broken painted lines placed a weight beneath his heart that threatened to sink him.

When she let go of his hand he felt a twinge of regret, but with the fading of strange sensations he recovered his purpose somewhat. The pictures on the wall were not much, but when he made his recommendations he would certainly reference them. Whether it was the incongruous angles at which they had been hanged or the subjects themselves, they brought disorder and menace to an otherwise perfectly pleasant summer hallway.

Following her lead as she bounced into the kitchen at the back of the house, he was almost overcome by the rich scent that greeted him. Unable to identify what it came from, certain that he had never smelled its like before, he stopped dead a few steps into the cosy room. The aroma had a texture, which stroked the inside of his nose and mouth with musky sweetness, and piled up heavily behind his eyes.

Suddenly he was very sleepy indeed.

"Here's your coffee," she said, passing him a mug. "You should drink it while you look out of the window."

There was nothing objectionable about her suggestion, and he found

himself leaning next to the sink, staring down into a field behind the house. There was a distant shed, and a fence with flaking white paint on the boards. An old fashioned child's bicycle with a rich matte green frame was propped against the fence. Though a little scratched, it was for the most part in excellent condition. Only the seat aged it, for the tan leather had been shredded and dangled in torn flaps. It looked like a vicious, animalistic wound, as though the bike had been stalked and pounced upon.

The grass on which the bike sat was a stiff, dead brown.

Blinking, he sipped his coffee to clear his head. It was black and bitter, as he liked it, but there was an under-taste that shot childhood fear through his guts. Tequila and cigars, a familiar cocktail. He remembered things he had not thought on for many years. Infant things, and not so infant. Tequila and cigars.

The scene through the window was faded and strange, as though he was looking at it through sepia stained glass. Lowering his mug to the counter, afraid he would tremble and drop it, he tried to blink the image to more modern life. "What… what is that?"

She moved up behind him, so close he could feel her warmth, and her voice was small and sad. "That was the day I died. I like to keep it handy." There was a shadow by the shed, that coiled with thick need. Its focus was the bicycle, he was certain, but it made no break to approach it over the grass. That was a good thing. The shadow scared him in ways that he was unable to articulate, even within the comfort of his own head.

"Was it your bicycle?"

"Yes. I died on it. When did you die?"

"I… I didn't." He was very tired and very cold, able to manage no more than a whisper. The taste of tequila and cigars banged through his throat every time he swallowed.

"I think you did. I think we all did. There is a moment when you know who you are and what the world is and what you're going to be, and then there is another in which you discover that you are wrong. It happened to everyone. We all died."

"Not me."

"Then why aren't you the person you thought you would be?" Fingers rested on his shoulder, brushing the hairs on the back of his neck like a cat's tongue. "We're still waiting to be born. Living, learning, waiting for the next moment when we understand it all." If he turned, he thought he might see her naked, so he stared with renewed intensity at the bike and the shadow. As horrible a statement of things gone by as they were, he was more frightened that she might be exposed now. She contained things he did not want to understand.

"Come to bed," she said, as the sun touched the horizon. Others may have had the will to resist her, but he could not.

***

He woke beside her on the bed, still in his grey suit and his shiny black shoes. It was dark, and he could not see her. When she shifted on the mattress he could tell that she was very much larger than she had been earlier. Something soft and fibrous brushed his arm. Flat on his back, he twitched a hand and stroked it.

While he slept she had wrapped herself in living silk and become a chrysalis. He was so envious that he started to cry. Tequila and cigars. How long would he have to wait?

***

In the morning he woke to an empty bedroom, and understood that he would never see her tropical eyes again. It made him very sad, but happy too. After many years of waiting, she wasn't dead anymore. It would be his turn, someday. The house belonged to him, and he belonged to the house. The view from the kitchen would be different when he went downstairs, and he was nervous about that. It needed to be stared at though. He needed to see the day he died.

The paintings in the hallway had also changed by the time he descended to view them. The scenes were familiar, and made him ache. There was coffee waiting for him on the kitchen counter. He drank it as he looked out of the window, refilling it to the brim with his own tears after every sip.

It tasted of tequila and cigars, and he thought it would do so until the next time he was born.

The Four Horsemen Would Like to Thank Our MINIONS:

Michelle Erb

Kevin Lucia

Kira Trudell

Candace Yost

We Honestly Couldn't do this Without YOU!

Author Sponsors

Rena Mason is a Bram Stoker Award winning author of The Evolutionist and East End Girls, as well as a 2014 Stage 32 / The Blood List presents: The Search for New Blood Screenwriting Contest Finalist. A longtime fan of horror, sci-fi, science, history, historical fiction, mysteries, and thrillers, she began writing to mash up those genres in stories revolving around everyday life. She is a member of the Horror Writers Association, Mystery Writers of America, International Thriller Writers, and The International Screenwriters' Association. She writes a column for the HWA's Monthly Newsletter "Recently Born of Horrific Minds" and has written a handful of articles. Rena also volunteers in other roles with the organization, event planner the most recent acquisition. An avid SCUBA diver since 1988, she has traveled the world and enjoys incorporating the experiences into her stories. She currently resides in Reno, Nevada with her family.

Andrew Wolter is the award-winning author of the books Much of Madness, More of Sin, and Nightfall. His short stories have appeared in several anthologies, as well as print and online publications. Andrew's friendly and uncensored interaction with his readers has gained him a vast following among the social networks. Although he is predominantly known for writing horror, Andrew identifies himself as an author without genre limitations. Though he always conveys a realistic moral in his fiction, Andrew's tales remain dark and without remorse. Readers will find that all of Andrew's works contain both gay and straight characters. The development of such characters is nothing more than art imitating life and a knowledge of what he has experienced. In addition to his fiction writing, Andrew has freelanced as a contributing columnist to various magazines. He has over 85 published reviews and over 15 published interviews. Being a strong advocate for human rights, he also freelances as a contributing columnist (under the name Tristan Wilde) for a several LGBT publications. Though Andrew was born in St. Louis, Missouri, he has spent a majority of his childhood and adulthood in Phoenix, Arizona. A current resident of Seattle, Washington, Andrew is an active member of the Horror Writers Association and is currently working on several forthcoming books.

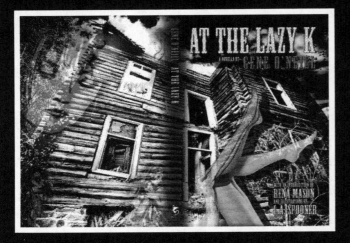

Surprise Guests

Gak is an artist/gypsy who can't seem to stay in one place very long. Fortunately Gak discovered a career that enables him to bounce around the country on a whim. One might think this is clever planning but is really just blind luck. gak has worked with some of the best publishers in the small press arena including Cemetery Dance, Necro Publications, Delirium Books, Thunderstorm Books and Written Backwards...with gak's work appearing alongside such greats as Edward Lee, Jack Ketchum, Brian Keene, Gene O'neill and Robert Sawyer...to name just a few. gak apologizes for the gratuitous use of the name gak during this bio.

Gord Rollo was born in St. Andrews, Scotland, but now lives in Ontario, Canada. His short stories and novella-length work have appeared in many professional publications throughout the genre and his novels include: The Jigsaw Man, Crimson, Strange Magic, and Valley Of The Scarecrow. His work has been translated into several languages and his titles are currently being adapted for audiobooks

F. Paul Wilson is the author of more than forty books: science fiction (HEALER, WHEELS WITHIN WHEELS, AN ENEMY OF THE STATE, DYDEETOWN WORLD, THE TERY, SIMS), horror thrillers (THE KEEP, THE TOMB, THE TOUCH, REBORN, REPRISAL, NIGHTWORLD, BLACK WIND, SIBS, MIDNIGHT MASS), contemporary thrillers (THE SELECT, IMPLANT, DEEP AS THE MARROW), novels that defy categorization (THE FIFTH HARMONIC, VIRGIN) and a number of collaborations. In 1998 he resurrected his popular antihero, Repairman Jack, and has chronicled his adventures in LEGACIES, CONSPIRACIES, ALL THE RAGE, HOSTS, THE HAUNTED AIR, GATEWAYS, CRISSCROSS, INFERNAL, HARBINGERS, BLOODLINE, BY THE SWORD, GROUND ZERO, and FATAL ERROR.

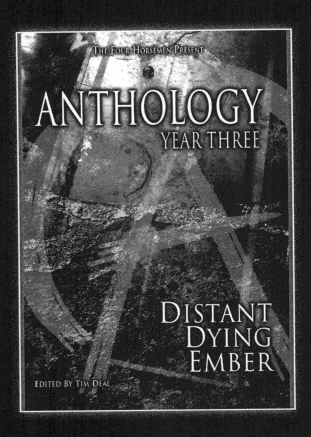

THE FOUR HORSEMEN PRESENT

ANTHOLOGY
YEAR THREE

DISTANT DYING EMBER

EDITED BY TIM DEAL

A wildly adventurous collection of stories and verse that cross the thresholds of genre. Here you'll find epic battles as the forces of order combat alien extremism in space; the confrontation between Norse Gods and the almighty Cthulhu; and otherworldly invaders causing havoc by controlling the elements. But there's much more. In these 29 well-crafted pieces of prose, verse, and artwork, there are more subtle moments: cozy mysteries, time travel, apparitions on lonely highways, isolation, and moments of nail-biting suspense. Over 300 pages of exciting and startling fiction, verse, and art. Written and compiled from the authors, artists, and poets that have been guests at the Anthology Conference (AnthoCon) in historical Portsmouth, NH, DISTANT DYING EMBER represents a colorful and intense journey into the psyches of a talented group of people from all over the world.

Made in the USA
Middletown, DE
27 May 2015